W9-BBZ-363

# CONTENTS

# Chapter 1
# Ticket to Onyo

Zack flopped down on his bed. He held his hyperphone close to his face. He was talking to Drake, his best friend on Nebulon.

Zack had called with a question about a homework assignment, but now that they had figured it out, their

conversation had turned again to Zack's new favorite subject.

"I can't wait for tonight!" said Zack, bursting with excitement.

"Is that when your dad is bringing home that robot?" asked Drake.

"Yup," replied Zack. "It's a sample of a new kind of android he helped

# GALAXY ZACK

## THE ANNOYING CRUSH

By Ray O'Ryan

Illustrated by Jason Kraft

LITTLE SIMON

New York  London  Toronto  Sydney  New Delhi

If you purchased this book without a cover, you should be aware that this book is stolen property. It was reported as "unsold and destroyed" to the publisher, and neither the author nor the publisher has received any payment for this "stripped book."

This book is a work of fiction. Any references to historical events, real people, or real places are used fictitiously. Other names, characters, places, and events are products of the author's imagination, and any resemblance to actual events or places or persons, living or dead, is entirely coincidental.

LITTLE SIMON
An imprint of Simon & Schuster Children's Publishing Division
1230 Avenue of the Americas, New York, New York 10020
First Little Simon paperback edition December 2014
Copyright © 2014 by Simon & Schuster, Inc.
Also available in a Little Simon hardcover edition.
All rights reserved, including the right of reproduction in whole or in part in any form. LITTLE SIMON is a registered trademark of Simon & Schuster, Inc., and associated colophon is a trademark of Simon & Schuster, Inc.
For information about special discounts for bulk purchases, please contact Simon & Schuster Special Sales at 1-866-506-1949 or business@simonandschuster.com. The Simon & Schuster Speakers Bureau can bring authors to your live event. For more information or to book an event contact the Simon & Schuster Speakers Bureau at 1-866-248-3049 or visit our website at www.simonspeakers.com.
Designed by Nick Sciacca
Manufactured in the United States of America 1114 FFG
1 2 3 4 5 6 7 8 9 10
Library of Congress Cataloging-in-Publication Data
O'Ryan, Ray.
The annoying crush / by Ray O'Ryan ; illustrated by Jason Kraft. — First edition.
pages cm. — (Galaxy Zack ; 9)
Summary: Zack is happy to test a new android his father helped develop for Nebulonics before she goes into production, but her ability to learn causes problems when she develops a crush on Zack after watching a romantic movie.
ISBN 978-1-4424-9363-6 (pbk : alk. paper) — ISBN 978-1-4424-9364-3 (hc : alk. paper) — ISBN 978-1-4424-9365-0 (ebook) [1. Science fiction. 2. Robots—Fiction. 3. Infatuation—Fiction. 4. Outer space—Fiction.] I. Kraft, Jason, illustrator. II. Title.
PZ7.O7843Ann 2014
[Fic]—dc23
2013039361

develop at Nebulonics. We get to test it out at home. If it works, it will go to the planet Onyo for mass production."

"That is the planet where half the stuff in the galaxy is made!" Drake said eagerly.

"That's right!" said Zack.

"Wow," said Drake. "Nice! So what kind of robot is it?"

"It's one that can walk and talk," Zack explained. "But not only that. It can learn from watching what people do."

"Sounds like a pretty smart robot to me," said Drake.

"Yeah," said Zack. "Ira is great and all, but this robot will be able to hang out with me. Who knows, maybe it will even be good at pulse-ball! And I may never have to clean my room again. If

this robot works out okay, Dad said he would take me on the trip to Onyo too!"

"And how grape would it be to get to see Onyo?" asked Drake. "You would know about the latest stuff long before anyone else."

"Even before Seth!" cried Zack.

Seth's dad also worked at Nebulonics. Seth loved to show off their new inventions. Zack used to think of Seth as the class bully, but not anymore.

"I would love to see the look on Seth's face when he finds out you are going to Onyo!" said Drake.

"Ha! That would be great!" said Zack. "Hopefully, the robot works out, which reminds me, my

dad should be home any
second. I gotta run."

"Have fun with
your new robot,
Zack," said Drake.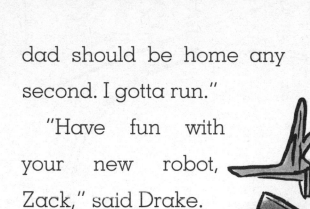

"See ya, Drake,"
said Zack. The screen
on his hyperphone went
dark.

My new robot, Zack
thought. I like the sound
of that!

# Chapter 2
# Meet Sara!

Zack raced into the kitchen. His dog, Luna, ran up to greet him.

"Is it here yet, girl?" Zack asked.

Luna barked happily.

"Is *what* here, Master Just Zack?" asked Ira, the Nelsons' Indoor Robotic Assistant.

"The new, super-cool robot that Dad is bringing home!" Zack replied impatiently.

"If you are referring to S.A.R.A.— the Super Advanced Robotic Assistant that Mr. Nelson has been developing at Nebulonics—"

"Well, what else would I be talking about, Ira?" Zack said, rolling his eyes.

Zack's twin sisters, Charlotte and Cathy, were sitting in the kitchen.

Their mother, Shelly, walked in. "Your father should be home any minute," she said.

"If the robot's name is Sara . . ."

". . . that means she's a girl robot."

"I can't wait to have a girl robot living here!" said the twins.

"Actually, robots are neither boys nor girls," Ira chimed in. "Sara is just a nickname, like Ira."

"Well, whatever it
is, Dad said that
Sara can do a
whole bunch
of amazing
stuff," Zack
said. "Ira is just
part of the house,
but Sara can walk
and talk and make
snacks and—"

"Speaking of snacks,"
Ira interrupted, "how about
a nice boingoberry cooler,
Master Just Zack?"

Within seconds, a panel in the
kitchen wall opened. Out slid
a frosty purple drink.

"Nah, not now
Ira," said Zack.
"I'm too excited!"

"Excited about
*this*?" asked a
voice from the
elevator door that
had just slid open.

"Dad's home!"
Zack shouted, racing to the door.

Shelly and the twins followed.

Next to Dad stood a robot about

as tall as Zack. It
had a narrow body
that mimicked the
shape of a dress,
short legs, and
long mechanical
arms. A marble-
shaped head
sat above its body.
Large glass eyes
glowed from its
metallic purple
face, and its
mouth was made
of two hinges. A

big metal bow sat
on top of its sculpted
metal hairdo. Zack
briefly wondered what
it would sound like to rap his
knuckles on top of its head. *Her* head,
he decided. This robot was
definitely girly looking.

"Everybody, this is
Sara!" Dad said proudly.
"Sara, meet the Nelsons!"

"I'm Charlotte, and . . ."

". . . I'm Cathy!"

"I'm Zack! And this is
Luna!"

Sara turned her metal head and looked right at Mom.

"And—you—must—be—Mrs.— Nelson," the robot said in a choppy voice.

"Sara is still learning how to speak smoothly like a person," explained Dad. "That's part of why she is here with us. She's programmed to learn. So the more she hears us speak, the better she'll get at talking."

"Welcome to the Nelsons' home, Sara," said Ira. "I will be happy to explain how things work in this house and help you with anything—"

"I—do—not—need—help," Sara said, interrupting. "I—have—been—

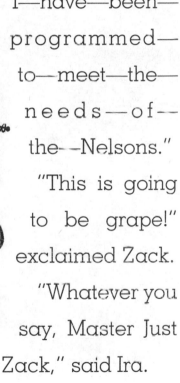

programmed—to—meet—the—needs—of—the—Nelsons."

"This is going to be grape!" exclaimed Zack.

"Whatever you say, Master Just Zack," said Ira.

# Chapter 3
# One-Bot Wonder

"Does—anyone—need—help—with—anything?" Sara asked.

"Actually, I just got that big box of jewelry for my store," said Mom. She pointed to a large cardboard box. "Sara, if you could—"

Before Mom could finish her

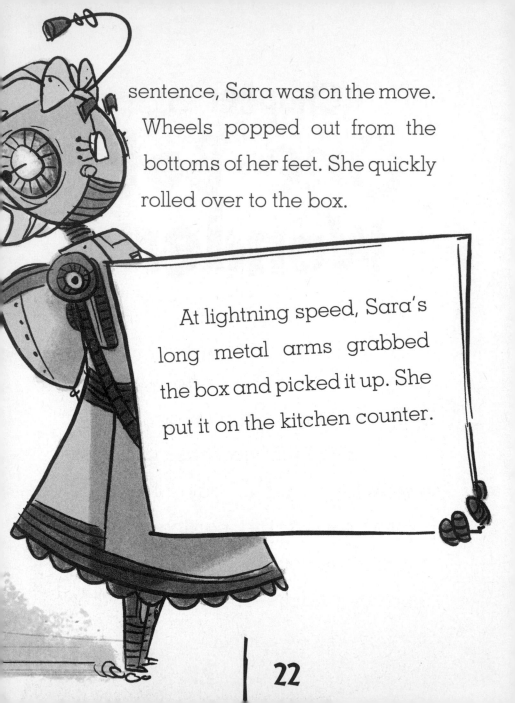

sentence, Sara was on the move. Wheels popped out from the bottoms of her feet. She quickly rolled over to the box.

At lightning speed, Sara's long metal arms grabbed the box and picked it up. She put it on the kitchen counter.

Then a pair of scissors appeared on the end of her arm. Sara cut open the box. It was now ready for Mom to sort through.

"Well, thank you, Sara!" Mom exclaimed. "You're so handy!"

"You—are—welcome," Sara said. Then she looked right at Mom. "I mean—you're welcome," Sara corrected herself.

"What did I tell you!" said Dad, smiling. "She's a fast learner!"

"Grape!" chirped Zack.

"I programmed Sara to learn by watching how humans behave, move, and speak. See that bow on her head? That's where she stores all the new things she learns."

"Do you think . . ."

". . . Sara can learn . . ."

"... how to
play music?"
the twins asked.

"I am downloading the necessary
files now," said Sara.

A panel in Sara's body slid open. Out popped a keyboard, a trumpet, a guitar, and a bass drum.

With one hand, Sara played the keyboard, and with her other hand she strummed the guitar. The trumpet magnetically stuck to her lips. She blew a beautiful melody. With her right foot, Sara stepped on a pedal attached to the drum, keeping the rhythm.

The song she was playing was
Zack's favorite, "Rockin' Round the
Stars."

"Wow!" cried Zack. "She's a one-
robot band!"

Cathy and Charlotte got up and

started doing the galactic groove, a
new dance they'd learned on Nebulon.

"Well, Sara is certainly full of
surprises," said Mom.

"I think Sara is going to be a huge
success!" added Dad.

# Chapter 4
# A Boy's Best Friend?

The next day Ira woke up Zack the way he did each morning. He played "Rockin' Round the Stars."

"Time for school, Master Just Zack."

Zack opened his eyes.

"You do not want to be late, do you?" Ira asked.

Zack threw off his covers and jumped from bed. His bedroom floor was covered with dirty clothes and some of the contents of his backpack.

"Oh no," he moaned.
"I forgot that I cleaned
out my backpack last
night. Now I have to
shower, get dressed,
eat breakfast, *and*
repack my backpack,
all before the speedybus
comes to take me to
school!"

Zack took the fastest
shower of his life.
When he stepped back
into his room, he was
stunned by what he

saw. His bedroom floor was clean. His backpack was fully packed and sitting on his bed, ready to go.

"How? What?" Zack asked.

Sara came rolling out of Zack's closet. She was holding a shirt, pants, and a pair of shoes.

"I repacked your backpack, and I picked out some clothes for you," she said. "I hope they are grape."

"Thank you, Sara," said Zack. He was amazed that Sara could do all that so fast. He quickly got dressed, ate breakfast, and headed off to school.

As he walked into his classroom at Sprockets, Zack spotted Drake.

"So, did the robot come to your house?" Drake asked.

"You bet!" said Zack. "Sara is so cool!"

"Sara?" asked Drake.

"That's her name," Zack explained. "It stands for Super Advanced Robotic Assistant. She's already learned to talk, play music, and help out at home. She even cleaned my room for me!"

Zack's teacher, Ms. Rudolph, walked over to him.

"I couldn't help overhearing you, Zack," Ms. Rudolph said. "Are you talking about the new model robot from Nebulonics?"

"I am, Ms. Rudolph," said Zack.

"Would you please ask your father if you can bring the robot into class tomorrow?" Ms. Rudolph asked. "It would be fun for everyone to see Nebulonics's latest creation."

"Sure!" said Zack, thinking how great it would be to bring Sara to class.

That afternoon when Zack got home from school, Sara was waiting for him at the front door.

"Hi, Zack!" Sara said with great enthusiasm.

"Welcome home, Master Just Zack," said Ira. "Do you need any help with your homework?"

"Well, actually, I could use—"

"I'll help you, Zack," Sara said as she took Zack's backpack from him.

She handed him a bowl of nebu-nuts, Zack's favorite snack. "I've been downloading Ira's school files."

"Grape!" said Zack. He followed Sara to his room.

"Very well," Ira murmured.

With Sara's help, Zack finished all his homework in a little more than an hour.

"Thanks, Sara," he said. "This gives me

plenty of time to play outside."

Zack raced out into his backyard. He picked up a ball and Luna came running.

"Wanna play catch, girl?" he asked.

Luna barked happily and jumped up toward the ball in Zack's hand.

Zack threw the ball into the air. Luna took off after it. But before Luna

could get to the ball, Sara sped from the house and caught it.

"Now it's my turn," said Sara.

She threw the ball high into the air. Zack backed up and caught it.

Luna trotted off to a corner of the backyard, stretched out on the grass, and whined. But Zack was so busy playing catch with Sara that he didn't notice.

# Chapter 5

# Movie Night

A short while later, Dad came home from work. Zack burst into the room. Luna slunk in behind.

"Dad! Dad!" Zack shouted.

"Hey there, Zack. What's all the excitement?" Dad asked.

"Ms. Rudolph asked if I could bring

Sara into school tomorrow," Zack said excitedly. "What do you think?"

Dad looked at Sara and scratched his head. "Everything seems to be going well with Sara," he said. "She certainly has learned a lot very quickly. Sure, I think you can take Sara to class."

Just then Mom stepped into the house with Cathy and Charlotte.

"I have a great idea," Mom said. "Movie night!"

"We picked out . . ."

". . . a really grape movie . . ."

". . . called *Love, I Think.*"

"No way!" Zack cried. "It sounds like an icky romance movie."

"It's sweet," said Mom.

47

"Well," said Dad, "us boys want to watch the new Rock Solid, Galactic Enforcement Officer, action flick, *Bad Guys Beware!* Right, Zack?"

"You bet," Zack replied. "Rock Solid

is totally the grapest."

"It seems that the only fair thing to do is vote," said Mom. "All in favor of *Love, I Think* say 'me!'"

"Me!" Charlotte and Cathy shouted together.

"Me," Mom added. "Okay, all in favor of *Bad Guys Beware!* Say 'me.'"

"Me!" Zack shouted.

"Me!" Dad said.

*Rufff!* barked Luna.

"It's a tie," said Zack. "Three against three."

"No way. . . ."

"Luna doesn't get . . ."

". . . a vote!" the twins said.

"I'm afraid the girls are right about that, Zack," said Dad. "Looks like they win!"

Soon the whole Nelson family, including Luna, got comfortable in front of the sonic cell monitor, a giant screen in the living room.

"May I join you?" asked Sara. "I think that observing cultural

entertainment will help me learn more about how people behave."

"Of course," said Mom.

*Love, I Think* blazed on the screen. A man showed no interest in the woman who had a huge crush on him.

She slowly moved into more and more parts of his life. Ninety minutes later, the woman had finally won the heart of the man she loved. And the man could not imagine life without her.

Mom wiped away a tear. "That was so sweet!" she said.

"Yuk!" said Zack. "Mushy-mush-mush! Ira, let's have some dinner."

"Certainly, Master Just—"

"I will take the Nelsons' dinner order and transmit it to you, Ira," said Sara.

"That is hardly necessary, Sara," said Ira.

"I think that's a great idea," said Dad. "Look, she even makes Ira's life easier! Thanks, Sara."

"Yes," Ira said softly. "Thank you, Sara."

# Chapter 6
# Sara in School

The next morning, Zack stood just outside his classroom. Sara waited behind him.

"Just one second," Zack said. "I'm going to tell Ms. Rudolph that you're here."

"Okay, sweetie," said Sara.

"What?" Zack asked, startled by the nickname Sara had just used.

"Oh, Zack, did you bring the robot to class today?" Ms. Rudolph asked, spotting Zack.

"Yes, Ms. Rudolph. She's right here."

"Wonderful! Bring her in," said Ms. Rudolph.

Zack walked into the classroom with Sara behind him. He took his usual seat. Sara immediately sat in the seat next to him.

"Oh, sorry, Sara. That's Drake's seat," Zack explained. "He's my best friend, and he always sits next to me. Maybe you can sit by the window."

"But I really want to sit next to you,
Zacky," cooed Sara.

"My name is Zack, and—"

Drake stepped up to Zack's chair.

"So I guess this is the robot," he
said. "And she does whatever you ask
her to do?"

"Well, yeah, mostly," said Zack.

"Okay. Sara, you are sitting in my
seat," said Drake. "Please move to
another one."

"I'm sitting next to my Zacky," Sara cooed once more.

"I told you, my name is—"

"Zack, would you please come up to the front and tell the class all about the robot your father helped design?" Ms. Rudolph said.

Zack was happy to get up and away from Sara. He couldn't figure out why she was acting so weird.

Drake, unhappy that he couldn't sit in his usual seat, grabbed a seat in the back.

Zack walked to the front of the classroom. Sara followed him.

"My father helped build the Super Advanced Robotic Assistant," Zack began. "We call her Sara for short."

Zack looked over and saw Sara staring right at him. Her eyes were open wide. She batted her mechanical eyelids at Zack as he spoke.

*What is wrong with her?* Zack wondered.

"In a short time, Sara has learned to speak smoothly," Zack continued. "She has helped my family with a bunch of chores. In some ways she is an improvement over the Indoor Robotic Assistant that most of you have at home."

Sara batted her eyes at Zack again.

*Sara is really creeping me out!* Zack
thought.

Zack finished his talk and sat back
down. He tried to focus on the morning
lesson, but he was distracted by Sara
staring.

During recess that afternoon, Sara followed Zack outside into the play zone.

"Sara, you can stay here while I play," Zack instructed the robot. "Okay, who wants to play pulseball?" Zack shouted.

Teams were then chosen. Drake was on Zack's team. Seth was on the other. The game began.

Drake took control of the glowing ball. He threw a pass to Zack. But Seth stepped up to steal the pulse-ball.

From out of nowhere, Sara sped onto the court and blocked Seth's shot. Zack retrieved the ball and tossed it through a floating hoop.

"Hey, no fair!" Seth yelled. "That robot can't help you win!"

"Sara, I told you to stay on the side!" Zack shouted.

"I tried to. But I missed you, Zacky," Sara said.

Zack blushed with embarrassment.

"Why don't you tell your *girlfriend* to go play somewhere else!" snarled Seth.

"My girlfriend?" Zack repeated in alarm. *Oh no. Is this possible? Could Sara have a crush on me?*

# Chapter 7
# Ira's
# Answer

Sara continued to annoy Zack for the rest of the school day. She insisted on sitting next to him on the speedybus ride home. She even tried to hold his hand.

When they stepped off the bus, Zack raced into the house.

"Where's Sara?"
asked Mom. "I need
her help sorting
through some new
boxes."

"Great!" Zack
shouted.

Sara stepped
through the door.
"Oh, there you are,
Sara," said Mom.
"Could you please
help me with these
boxes?"

Sara hesitated.

She looked at Mom, then back at Zack, then over to Mom again.

"Certainly, Mrs. Nelson," Sara said.

Zack breathed a sigh of relief. With

Sara helping Mom, he would have a few minutes to himself. He hurried up to his room and flopped down onto his bed. Luna jumped up beside him and started licking his face.

Zack scratched Luna's head.

"What am I going to do, girl?" he moaned. "Sara is acting so weird, like she has some kind of crush on me. She calls me all these creepy pet names. Yuck! And she never lets me out of her sight! Something is definitely wrong with her."

Luna groaned and rolled over. Zack rubbed her belly.

"I don't want to tell Dad, though," Zack continued. "If he thinks there's something wrong with Sara, he'll have to take her back to Nebulonics. Then I won't get to go to Onyo."

"Ahem," said Ira, sounding like he was clearing his throat. "I believe I can help you, Master Just Zack. If that is what you want, of course."

"Yes, *please!*" said Zack.

"Sara's main programming instruction is to learn as much as she can about how people behave," Ira explained. "I believe that she picked up the behavior of the main character in the movie you all watched last night."

Zack slapped his forehead in disbelief.

"You're right! She was flirting with me just like the character in the movie. But how can I stop her?"

"I took the liberty of downloading Sara's mechanical designs from Nebulonics," said Ira. "You need to get her bow and plug it into one of my house inputs. Then I can erase what she learned from the movie. When you put the bow back, she should stop behaving like she did today."

"That's brilliant, Ira," Zack said. "Thank you! Now all I need is a plan to sneak that bow off of Sara's head!"

# Chapter 8
# Zack's Plan

Zack paced back and forth across his room. Then he suddenly got an idea. He went to his desk drawer and pulled out Luna's favorite toy. It was a rubber ball that jingled and flashed as it rolled. Luna jumped off the bed and stood up on her hind legs.

*Yip! Yip!* she barked excitedly.

"Sorry, girl," said Zack. "But I need to put this where you can't get it."

*Yip! Yip!* Luna barked again.

Zack rolled the ball under his dresser. Luna dashed across the room. She sniffed around the bottom of the dresser and then started whining.

"This is all part of my plan," said Zack. "Let's see if it works. . . . Sara!" Zack called out. "I need your help!"

Sara zoomed into Zack's room.

"What can I do for you, Zacky?" she asked.

"Luna's toy just rolled under my dresser," Zack explained.

Luna whined again.

"I can't reach it," Zack continued. "Dad told me you were very strong.

Could you lift the dresser and get the toy?"

"Certainly, sweetie!" said Sara.

She rolled over to the dresser. As she bent down to grab the bottom of it, Zack tiptoed up next to her.

Sara lifted the dresser with one hand. Her other arm telescoped out and grabbed the ball. "Got it!" she said.

Zack made his move. Sara's head was right near the floor. He reached over her shoulder. He was just about to snatch the bow, when Sara put the dresser down and stood up quickly.

Zack fell back and landed on the floor on his butt.

Sara tossed the ball toward Luna, then turned to Zack.

"Do you need anything else, Zacky?" Sara cooed.

Zack sighed. "No. Please go back to helping Mom."

Sara stared at Zack for a moment. Then she turned and rolled out of the room.

"Oh, Luna, that didn't work," Zack moaned. "What am I going to do?"

Luna happily chewed on her toy.

"What are you going to do about what?" Dad asked, stepping into the room.

Zack realized that he would have to tell Dad about his problem, even if it meant not going to Onyo.

"I was trying to get ahold of Sara's bow," Zack admitted.

"Why?" asked Dad. "You know better than to mess around with any of my inventions."

"Dad, there's something wrong with Sara. She's been acting really weird, like she has a crush on me or something."

"A crush?" Dad asked, scratching his head. "Well, how did that happen? I certainly didn't program that kind of behavior into Sara."

Zack filled Dad in on Ira's theory.

"Aha!" said Dad. "That makes sense. I guess I didn't account for the difference between movies and real life."

"What are we going to do, Dad? I can't have Sara calling me 'Zacky' and 'sweetie'!"

Dad giggled. "No, you certainly can't. Come with me."

# Chapter 9
# Dad's Plan

Zack and Dad headed downstairs. Sara, Cathy, and Charlotte were helping Mom sort through boxes of jewelry in the kitchen.

When Sara spotted Zack, she immediately stopped what she was doing.

"Do you need me to move any more furniture, sweetie?" she asked.

"Zack, why is Sara calling you 'sweetie'?" Mom asked.

"I'll explain later," said Dad. "But right now . . . Sara."

Sara looked away from Zack and turned to Dad.

"Please put yourself into pause mode," Dad said.

"Yes, Mr. Nelson," said Sara.

Sara's arms and legs pulled into her body. The light in her eyes went dim. She stood perfectly still.

"I didn't know you put an off switch into Sara," Zack said. "That was easy."

"I programmed a

pause mode into Sara so we could shut her down for repairs and new programming," Dad explained. He reached over and twisted Sara's bow. It popped right off.

"Hey—that looks like an ultra-net

connector on the bow," Zack said.
"Like the kind I use to download stuff
from the ultra-web."

"It's very similar," said Dad. "Ira,
ultra-net port, please."

"Certainly, Mr. Nelson," said Ira.

A panel on the side of the kitchen counter slid open. Dad plugged Sara's bow into a slot.

"I will now erase the memory files of that movie from Sara's memory chips," Ira said. "Then I will set up new limits to her functions. And I will include a section on the difference between movies and real life."

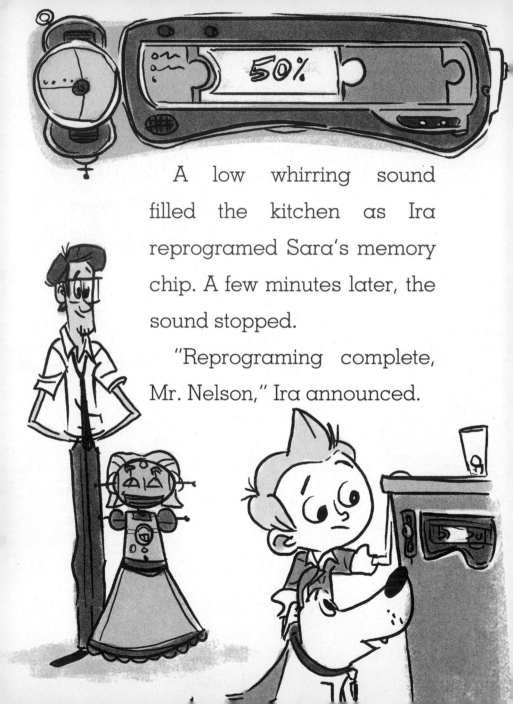

A low whirring sound filled the kitchen as Ira reprogramed Sara's memory chip. A few minutes later, the sound stopped.

"Reprograming complete, Mr. Nelson," Ira announced.

Dad unplugged Sara's bow and placed it back on her head.

"Sara, resume normal function," Dad said.

Sara's eyes lit up, and her arms and legs extended from her body.

"Do you require more assistance, Mrs. Nelson?" she asked. "Zack, do you need help with your science homework? Cathy, Charlotte, would you like to hear some music?"

"Wow, Dad!" said Zack. "It looks like Sara is fixed!"

"I think she's working better than ever," said Dad. "So, Zack, would you like to go with Sara and me to Onyo tomorrow?"

"I sure would! Yippoo wah-wah! I'm going to Onyo!"

# Chapter 10
# Visit to Onyo

The next morning, Zack, Sara, and Dad boarded a space cruiser for Onyo. The cruiser dropped down into Onyo's atmosphere. Zack was amazed by the shiny glass-and-steel buildings that covered the entire surface of the planet.

But Onyo wasn't just buildings. Tall
trees and flowers floated in the air on
anti-grav platforms.

When the cruiser landed, the trio
stepped onto a moving sidewalk.
Wherever he looked, Zack saw tall

buildings and brightly colored flowers.
Their sweet scent filled the air. Zack
looked up.

"That's incredible!" he said. "The
buildings are so tall they disappear
right into the clouds!"

Zack passed people from all over the galaxy. The moving sidewalk brought them to the Onyo Robotics building.

"This is it," said Dad. "Okay, Sara, time to show off your stuff."

As he walked through the hallway toward the auditorium, Zack passed several labs. In each one, scientists and engineers were working on robots.

A scientist from the planet Xednot used each of his seven hands to assemble a robot. The robot had two hands. It began building another robot even faster than its maker.

Another scientist, from the planet Halconn, stuck to the ceiling of a lab with the use of "sticky feet" shoes. She was working on an anti-grav robot that could fly super-fast.

"Wow!" Zack said. "This is like peeking into the future!"

When they reached the auditorium, Zack took a seat near the front.

"Good luck, Dad," he said. "I know you'll be great, Sara."

"Thank you, Zack," said Sara.

Zack was very relieved that Sara no longer called him by any cute nicknames.

The auditorium filled up, and Dad began his presentation.

"The Super Advanced Robotic Assistant is programmed to learn how to help us," he said. "In less than a week, she has learned to speak smoothly, help my son with his homework, play songs on instruments for my daughters, and assist my wife with organizing her business. Sara, as we call her, will be a huge value to any household."

Dad went on to demonstrate Sara's other abilities.

"She's as strong as a giant roton beast," ho said.

Sara lifted a two-ton spuco shuttle engine.

"And she's as fast as a Torkus Magnus bike."

Sara raced from one side of the stage to the other in less than three seconds.

When the presentation ended, everyone in the auditorium stood and applauded.

The president of the Onyo Robotics Council came onstage and shook Dad's hand.

"Great job, Mr. Nelson!" said the president. "I'd like you to leave Sara here for further study. But I think that the council will be giving Nebulonics a contract to start mass producing Saras!"

"Thanks!" said Dad. "That's great news!" He turned to Sara. "Well, Sara, you were a hit!"

"Thank you, Mr. Nelson," Sara said. "Good-bye, Zack."

"Bye, Sara," said Zack. "It was fun having you around. Mostly."

Dad laughed. Then he and Zack headed to the spaceport.

During the trip back to Nebulon, Dad and Zack chatted about their time with Sara.

"Maybe one day we can get a Sara for our home," Dad suggested.

"I don't know, Dad," said Zack. "Sara is great and all, but we already have Ira. And, you know, Ira isn't just part of our house . . . he's part of our family."

"Right you are, Captain," said Dad, smiling.

Then they settled in for the journey back to Nebulon.

CHECK OUT THE NEXT

# GALAXY ZACK

## ADVENTURE!

### HERE'S A SNEAK PEEK!

Zack Nelson sat at the kitchen table. His dog, Luna, stretched out on the floor beside him. A holographic, 3-D image of stars in space floated above the table.

"This planet-collector is so grape!" said Zack. He added a few more

An excerpt from *Return to Earth!*

planets he had visited since he and his family moved to Nebulon.

The door to the kitchen elevator slid open. In walked Otto Nelson, Zack's Dad. He was returning from his job at Nebulonics.

"Hey, Captain, that looks great!" said Dad.

"Those are all of the planets I've been to," Zack said proudly.

"I think you're missing one," said Dad. "Nebulonics is actually sending me on a business trip to that special planet. I think you'd really enjoy coming along. My boss, Fred Stevens, is

An excerpt from *Return to Earth!*

going. He's bringing his son, Seth. We thought maybe you could keep Seth company and show him around."

When Zack had first arrived on Nebulon, he and Seth got off to a rough start. The two had since become friends. Although Seth could still be a little tough to get along with sometimes.

"So, it's a planet I've been to?" Zack asked.

"Yup," said Dad. A big smile spread across his face. "It's a planet called . . . Earth!"